SAMANTHA
Hatches The Chicken Egg

by Daisy T. Griffin

illustrated by Matthew Gauvin

www.SamsAnimals.info

~Dedicated to Jeblan and Cassidy, who actually did ride around in a car to keep chicks warm on a cold, stormy night.~

Contents

Chapter 1

The Farm

"Look at all those feathers," Samantha told her best friend Gerti as she pointed out the car window.

"Oh my gosh, what is that thing?" Gerti replied. Samantha and Gerti had just pulled up to their 4-H meeting. The meeting was being held on a farm and both girls were really excited.

"That's a chicken, silly," Gerti's mom broke in.

"He looks more like a pom-pom," Gerti giggled.

Gerti's mom was dropping them off at the 4-H meeting. Samantha's mom was going to pick them up. Gerti and Samantha joined 4-H club this year. Today they were touring a local farm. Strutting around the farmyard was a fluffy chicken with lots of little bitty fluffy chicks running around its legs.

When they jumped out of the car they saw Sally standing by the barn. Sally was ten, two years older than Samantha and Gerti. She was the club historian and had her camera around her neck ready to take pictures of today's tour. Sally also lived on the farm.

Her parents, known as Farmer Joe and Miss Sal, owned the farm. As Sally walked over to say hi, Samantha and Gerti stopped to look at the chickens.

Sally snapped a picture of them just as the mother hen flapped her wings at Gerti.

"Hey Guys!" Sally greeted them, "I'm glad you could come. I have something I want to show you."

Samantha and Gerti followed Sally around the barn to a little pen with a shed in it. Inside the shed there was a lot of hay on the ground. Lying on the hay were a pair of twin baby goats taking a nap.

"They were just born last night," Sally whispered so she wouldn't disturb them.

Samantha thought whispering was a little silly since all the other goats in the pen were being loud anyway, but she whispered too when she said, "They are beautiful."

"So cute," Gerti quietly agreed.

Just then, Sally's little brother Josh and a group of boys all came running around the side of the barn. Josh pointed at the little goats and shouted out, "Right there, see!"

The little goats woke up with a start and began bleating loudly, "maaaaahhh, maaaahhh."

Sally rolled her eyes and pushed her little brother playfully. "Josh, you woke them up," Sally said.

"Yeah, well, now we can play with them," replied Josh. He was not remorseful.

"Wait a minute," Samantha told them. The mother goat had come over to her babies when they started crying and the babies were nudging her udder looking for milk. "The babies are hungry. Let them eat," Sam told the boys. Josh seemed to notice Samantha and Gerti for the first time.

"Oh, hi, Samantha. Hi, Gerti. How's Gayzer doing?" Josh asked.

"Hey Josh. He's good, I saw him last week," Samantha replied. Gayzer was a box turtle that Samantha had brought to school earlier in the year. It was during that adventure that she and Josh had become friends.

"Cool. Well, I'll catch you later. If we can't play with the goats, I'm gonna show these guys how to catch a chicken," Josh said. With that he ran off challenging the other boys to a game of see-who-can-catch-the-chicken.

There were chickens walking around free all over the farm. Some of them were small and fluffy like the ones they saw from the car. Others were large and white or dark rust colored, and the roosters had bright plumage of many colors. Pretty soon the chickens were running. The boys were laughing hysterically as one and then another bit the dust chasing chickens.

The girls ignored the boys and turned their attention back to the goat kids. As they watched, each baby found a nipple and started nursing hungrily. The mother goat didn't seem to mind and stood there munching on hay.

Just then, Miss Sal started calling everyone to gather up for the 4-H meeting. Samantha suspected the timing had more than a little bit to do with distracting the boys from their mayhem.

After the meeting was over the kids were allowed to wander around the farm until it was time for their parents to pick them up. Samantha and Gerti decided they

wanted to go back and see the baby goats
one last time.

While they were looking in the goat pen
Gerti noticed three white eggs were laying
in the edge of the hay.

"Look Samantha. What kind of eggs do
you think those are?" Gerti asked her friend.

Farmer Joe overheard her question as he
was walking by. "Those are chicken eggs.
Let's see, those nice white eggs come from

our white leghorns. They are the pretty white chickens you see over there. All of these chickens lay eggs all over the farm," he told the girls as he pointed to a couple of beautiful white hens.

"What will happen to them?" Samantha asked.

"Well" replied Farmer Joe thoughtfully, "There is no telling what will happen to those eggs around here. If you girls took them home and would incubate them they might just have a chance at hatching." Then he winked at her and walked away whistling a merry tune.

Samantha grinned, "Come on Gerti, let's see how many eggs we can find." Gerti and Samantha climbed the gate to the goat pen and started gathering eggs. First they picked up the three eggs they originally saw. After closer inspection in the back of the stalls and in the edges of the grass they found even more. All in all they came out with nine chicken eggs.

When Samantha's mom came to pick them up Samantha and Gerti were each cradling an arm full of eggs as if they were babies. As soon as she was in the van, Samantha said, "Mom, we need an incubator."

Chapter 2

An Incubator

Mom looked at them suspiciously. "An incubator?" she asked.

Gerti held her breath. Sam gathered her courage and said, "Yes, an incubator. We rescued eggs from the goat pen, but they'll only hatch if we put them in an incubator to keep them warm."

"Samantha, we don't have an incubator," Her mom replied.

"That's why we need one, obviously. Mom, we've never hatched chickens before and I really really want to. Please."

Gerti grabbed Samantha's hand and squeezed it tight as both girls waited to hear if Sam's Mom would help them out.

Bringing the eggs home had seemed like such a good idea at the farm, but right now it looked more likely they'd be eaten for breakfast than hatched. Sam's mom was quiet for a long moment. She looked at the girls in the rear-view mirror. Samantha looked back at her, silently pleading with her to help. Finally Mom said, "Even if we get an incubator, eggs are a lot of work. Once they hatch, baby chickens are more work. And once they grow up, we'll have to find a good home for them."

Samantha let out a whoop of joy.

"Thank you, Mom! Thank you, thank you!" Sam said.

"I didn't say..." Mom started to argue, but instead she just laughed and said, "I expect you to take good care of them."

"We will," both girls replied. They were grinning from ear to ear and thinking about playing with baby chicks.

They stopped at Samantha's house before they took Gerti home so they could drop off the eggs. Mom helped the girls carefully put them in an egg carton.

"Be sure you put the smaller end down." Mom told them. The girls very carefully followed the instructions. Then Samantha took the carton of eggs and set them on the ledge of the window. She knew that they needed to be warm to hatch and the sunny ledge of the window was the warmest spot in her house.

"Oh no," Mom told her. "We need to put them somewhere cool." Samantha gave her mom a doubtful look.

"Mom, they won't hatch if they are cool." Samantha argued.

"True," said Mom. "But they also won't hatch on a windowsill. It's not warm enough to tell the egg to make the chicken grow inside. That's why we need an incubator."

"Let's go get one then, before the eggs die Mom." Samantha said.

"Girls, do you know how many eggs a chicken lays in one day?" Mom asked. The girls shook their heads.

"One," Mom answered her own question and held up one egg. "Now, did you see any hens at the farm with baby chicks? How many chicks did one hen have?" she asked them.

"The hen we saw had lots of babies. Eight is what I counted but, they were running everywhere and kept hiding under their mom," Gerti replied. Samantha hadn't thought to count the chicks, but Gerti likes numbers. She always seemed to remember that sort of thing.

"Right," Mom said, "Hens only set on their eggs after they have a full nest of eggs. It takes a while to lay all those eggs. In the meantime the eggs laid first, sit and wait."

"Are you sure?" Samantha questioned one more time. What her mom was saying made sense, but she was feeling very protective of her eggs.

"Yes. We could save them for a week and they'd be fine, but we'll find an incubator as soon as we can," Mom assured her.

Samantha and Gerti decided that a
shady spot in the kitchen cabinets would be
the safest place for the eggs. Before they
left, Samantha got a bright pink post-it note
and wrote "Live Eggs - Do Not Eat!" on it
and put it on the carton. Just in case

someone like her dad came home
and thought they looked tasty.

After they dropped Gerti off at her
house, the search for the incubator was on.
Mom went by the feed store on the way
home to see if they had any incubators for
sale. They did, but it cost a lot of money.
Mom did not buy one.

"Mom, please!" Samantha begged as
they walked out of the store. "We have to
get an incubator for the eggs. You said you
would help us," Samantha reasoned.

"And I will, but we'll have to find
another way. Those incubators were very
expensive and we can't afford to spend that
kind of money on them," Mom replied
matter-of-factly.

Samantha groaned. "You could if you wanted to," she muttered under her breath. Unfortunately, Mom heard her.

"Samantha!" Mom exclaimed. She stopped walking and looked Samantha right in the eyes.

"You're right, I could get this incubator if I wanted to. But then the money I spent on it would be gone and I wouldn't have it when it came time to buy other things. Money is limited. We have to spend it wisely. Those incubators are too expensive, but we'll figure out another way. Don't worry."

Samantha felt sheepish, but then Mom grinned, held out her hand and said, "Let's go figure this out." Samantha grabbed her

Mom's hand and skipped out the store with her.

After that, they headed home. Luckily, Samantha's two younger sisters, Sophie and Michelle, were out at a park with her Dad so there were no distractions.

At home Mom started making phone calls...

- Maybe the University has one they'll let us borrow.

— Nope

- Maybe someone we know has an incubator.

— Nah

- Maybe we can find a cheaper one on the internet.

- Uh uh

- Maybe we can build one.

- Not happening

Idea after idea didn't work out for one reason or another. Finally Mom said, "I wonder if your Grandma still has that old incubator from when I was a kid."

Samantha sighed. Even if she did, Grandma lived too far away to get it from her. Mom called to ask anyway. When she hung up the phone Mom said, "Grandma is going to look in the storage shed and call us back."

Samantha could hardly stand the wait. She went to the cabinet where the eggs were being stored and opened the carton one more time. The chicken eggs varied a lot. There were three that looked like the kind of eggs Samantha saw at the store. Big and solid white. Then there were four that were just slightly smaller and a dark reddish brown color. The last two eggs were only half the size of the others and had a nice creamy color. It seemed crazy to think that those hard ovals filled with egg goo could really turn into chickens.

While Samantha was sitting there dreaming about little chicken heads poking out of eggs, the phone rang. Samantha listened closely to her Mom's end of the conversation, "Any luck? Oh wonderful...Well it's the best option we have...Would you mind? Samantha will be so pleased....Thanks Mom....Love you too...Bye."

Samantha was about to burst to know what was going on.

"Grandma found the old incubator and she's shipping it to us this afternoon," Mom said.

Samantha started jumping up and down and shouted, "Wahoo! We are going to hatch our eggs!"

"Samantha," Mom said, "Don't get too excited. Grandma says that the incubator is a little beat up, and it hasn't been turned on in years. Even if it was the best incubator in the world, every egg isn't meant to hatch. Sometimes things go wrong. I don't want you to think that this means we are done.

There is still a long way to go before we are counting chickens."

Samantha's mood wasn't dimmed. She just knew that she'd have babies out of those eggs. She had a good feeling about it.

Chapter 3

Waiting

The eggs sat in the cabinet for three days waiting for the incubator to arrive. During that time, Samantha and her five year old sister, Sophie, had taken them down and looked at them every chance they got. Gerti had also called and asked how they were doing every day. It was a hard wait. Finally on Tuesday afternoon when

Samantha's mom picked her up from school, she brought news that the incubator had arrived.

"I've already talked to Gerti's mom. She's going to drop Gerti off at our house in a little while so she can set up the incubator with you," Mom told Samantha.

"Yeeeeeess!" Samantha cried.

"Woohoo!" Sophie yelled.

"TooWoo!" Their two year-old sister Michelle joined in from the back seat.

When they got home Samantha and Sophie raced inside. Sitting on the table was a round Styrofoam incubator. Grandma had not been kidding when she said it was a little beat up. On the top portion of the incubator were plastic windows to let you look in on the eggs. The glue holding those windows on had long ago given up on keeping it together. Samantha's Mother had taken duct tape and taped it all back down. The final product looked pretty rough. Samantha looked at it skeptically. She was worried.

Mom came in behind them with Michelle in tow. She strapped Michelle into the booster seat at the table and gave her Cheerios to distract her. "I know it looks rough, but watch this," Mom said as she took the cord and plugged it in. A little red light on top turned bright red.

"It works!" Samantha said with relief. All of a sudden that duct tape covered incubator was looking a lot better.

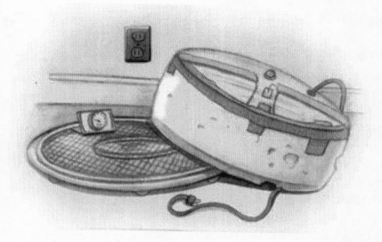

Mom put a thermometer inside it and
said to let it heat up to the right
temperature while they waited on Gerti.
Then she started cutting up apples for
snacks.

Samantha and Sophie could hardly wait.
They carefully took the carton of eggs out
of the cabinet and set it on the table. As
they started discussing who would get what

egg, Mom said, "Girls go and find three pencils please."

"Why?" Samantha and Sophie both asked.

"Because these little eggs need faces, of course," Mom said with a grin.

"We can't write on them!" Samantha responded. Sam thought maybe mom wasn't taking this responsibility of caring for the eggs as seriously as she should.

"Trust me, Samantha. You need pencils. Your eggs need to be marked. I'll explain it after Gerti gets here," Mom said.

Sophie was already rummaging through the pencil box in the closet. Sophie soon came back with three pencils. Two of them were sharpened.

"Oops," said Sophie when Samantha pointed out that one of them wouldn't write. Sophie ran and got another good pencil. As she was getting back, the doorbell rang.

"Gerti!" Samantha said and ran to let her friend in.

"Erti!" Michelle mimicked.

Gerti was anxious to see the eggs and followed Samantha over to the table. She wasn't too impressed with the looks of the incubator, but when Samantha's mom checked the thermometer it was 102 degrees Fahrenheit. The little incubator was hot!

"We need the temperature to be 101 degrees. I'm going to adjust the thermostat just a little bit," Mom said as she twisted a funny looking handle sticking up out of the top of the incubator. "Now, while we let that adjust I want each of you girls to mark one side of the eggs with those pencils," Mom said.

"Why would we draw on them?" asked Samantha.

"When a momma hen is setting on a nest she stands up every now and then and rolls the eggs around. This keeps the babies from sticking to one side of the shell or the other inside the egg. Since you guys are taking the place of the momma hen, you have to roll the eggs over. Putting a mark on one side of the egg lets you know which eggs you have already turned over," Mom replied.

"I think we would know anyway," Samantha countered.

"Ah, but when you have so many, sometimes it's hard to tell. And it's very important that they all get rolled over at least three times a day. Trust me Sam, this is how farmers do it all the time and the pencil doesn't hurt the chicks," Mom assured her.

"OK," Samantha relented, "I want to draw on this one and this one and this one." She pointed to one white egg and two reddish brown eggs.

"Ooh, I want this one and this one and this one and this one and this one," Sophie said, generally pointing at all the other eggs except one tiny one.

"Sophie! We each get three...that's fair!" Samantha scolded.

"Oh," Sophie said sheepishly, "Then I guess I'd like the other white eggs and a red one!"

Gerti smiled and said, "Works for me. I like the little bitty ones, and I'll take the last red one."

"Great, now you can draw whatever you want, but only write on one side of the egg," Mom instructed.

The girls went to work marking their eggs. Samantha just put an X on each of hers. She was still feeling like the less she marked on them, the better. Sophie put an S on her first egg, but then she looked over at Gerti who was drawing little faces on hers. Sophie drew smiley faces on her last two.

Mom checked the thermometer inside and it was 101 degrees Fahrenheit, just like she wanted. Mom then added water to a little well inside the incubator. "This is to keep the air inside humid," Mom explained, "If it gets too dry, the babies will dry up inside their shell and die. So we have to check the water every day and add more when it gets low."

"Yes, ma'am," the three girls replied.

"Es, am," Michelle added happily. She had stopped eating and was now just tossing Cheerios onto the floor.

Samantha, Sophie, and Gerti started to reach to put their eggs in the incubator.

"Not so fast," Mom stopped them, "Before you put those in, I want to make sure each of you understand that the chances of these eggs hatching out chicks is slim. The chances of *all* of these eggs hatching is almost none. There will be disappointment. Do you understand?" Mom looked at each of them.

The girls looked back and nodded, yes. Samantha thought her mom was being a little dramatic, but she agreed as fast as she could because she really wanted to get the eggs in the incubator.

"Make sure the side you marked is facing up," Mom told them as she finally lifted the lid just enough for them to each carefully lay their eggs inside. Samantha was happy when the eggs were safely in the warm incubator. Now to keep them safe until they could hatch.

Chapter 4

Refrigerator Egg

When Samantha went to turn the eggs before school the next morning there were more eggs in the incubator than the night before. The new eggs all had smiley faces on them.

"SOPHIE!" Samantha called.

"What?" Sophie answered.

"Why are there new eggs in the incubator?" Samantha asked.

"Oh, that. Weeeeelllll, I wanted more chickens. So I put in more eggs," Sophie said.

"Where did you get more eggs?"

"From the egg carton in the fridge."

"Sophie, those won't hatch," Samantha told her sister.

"Sure they will. They are chicken eggs. I marked them and everything," Sophie replied.

"Sophie, they aren't fertile. They can't make baby chickens."

"Baby chickens come from eggs...those are eggs." Sophie countered.

"The eggs that come from the store are from Momma chickens with no Daddy chickens. It takes a Momma **and** a Daddy to make baby chickens. If there is no Daddy, then we don't get any chicks. Make sense?"

"No."

"Just trust me, those won't hatch!" Samantha was getting exasperated and if they didn't hurry up they'd be late for school.

"Can we just leave one refrigerator egg in, just in case you are wrong?" Sophie begged.

"Fine, but it won't do anything," Samantha relented.

"Thanks," Sophie jumped up and gave Samantha a hug. Then she took out all but one of the refrigerator eggs. She tossed them in the compost pile in the backyard, and then hurried to make it to school.

Each day the eggs were carefully tended. Samantha turned the eggs every morning and checked the temperature and water inside the incubator. Mom turned the eggs at lunchtime while Sam and Sophie were at school. Sophie turned the eggs at night before bed. They had a large calendar on the wall where they had marked down what day they put the eggs in the incubator.

They also marked when the chicken eggs were due to hatch, 21 days later.

About a week after the eggs started incubating, Gerti came over to visit and check on the eggs one afternoon. Samantha lifted open the incubator lid so Gerti could peek inside.

"They look just the same. How do you know if it's working?" Gerti asked.

"I don't know. I guess we just wait and see if anything hatches," Samantha replied.

"What if we cracked one open a little bit?" Sophie offered. Samantha glared at her.

"And then taped it back together!" Sophie defended her idea.

Mom was walking by with the laundry

hamper full of clothes she was going to fold and stopped when she heard the girls talking.

"Hmm, I would candle the eggs if it were me," Mom said mysteriously and then walked on by and continued with her laundry.

"Candle the eggs?" Gerti said.

"Come on, let's look it up," Samantha replied. Sam knew what her mom was up to. She wanted them to figure it out for themselves. Samantha, Sophie and Gerti all went over to the computer that sat on a desk in the living room. Samantha pulled up Google search and typed in "candle chicken eggs". The first result that popped up was www.backyardchickens.com. It showed how to check and see if a chick was growing inside the egg using a flashlight.

The tutorial on the Internet showed how to take a piece of cardboard with a hole in it the size of a quarter and use it to cover up a light source. Then when you sat an egg over the hole, the light had to shine through the egg. This would illuminate what was inside and let you see shadows through the shell.

"Sophie, go get some cardboard out of the recycling bin. Gerti, you grab some scissors. I think I know where a light is that will work," Samantha directed.

Everyone ran to get the supplies and met back together in the living room. Samantha was carrying a lamp that was normally clamped to the side of her bed. "I thought you said we were going to *candle* the eggs. That's not a candle," Sophie pointed out to her older sister.

"A candle wouldn't be bright enough. Besides, you know we aren't allowed to play with fire by ourselves," Samantha told Sophie.

Sophie looked disappointed. She had been hoping for real fire. Oh well, it'd still be fun to see what was inside the eggs.

The first hole they cut was too big, the light shone out around the egg. The next hole they cut was small enough, but it was still hard to see much. Then Samantha remembered they were supposed to be in a dark room. She went and pulled the blinds

down and turned out all the lights in the living room.

"Hey!" Mom said, "I'm doing laundry in here."

"Mom, we just need it dark for minute. Wanna come see if we have babies in the egg?" Samantha replied.

Mom smiled, "Of course I do."

They very carefully took out the first chicken egg and placed it on the hole. It took a little maneuvering to get the light angled right, but pretty soon they were looking at a glowing egg. Inside the red glow within the egg, they could see a little black shadow that had dark veins spidering out from it.

"How wonderful, this one is growing! That little dark spot is a baby chicken forming," Mom told the girls.

"Yippee!" shouted Sophie.

"I knew it!" said Samantha.

"Whoa," whispered Gerti.

Samantha couldn't help the grin that was spreading across her face as she carefully set the chicken egg back into the incubator and grabbed the next egg. They candled each egg, and each time she was relieved to find the dark spot that meant a baby was growing inside. That is, until she got to the refrigerator egg that Sophie had snuck in. It was glowing red all over the inside. No dark spot to be found.

"Well, at least all the other eggs are fertile," Samantha said.

"Let's just keep it in a little longer to be sure," Sophie requested. Samantha sighed.

"OK, one more week Sophie," she agreed.

Chapter 5

Pee U!

The next morning Samantha opened the incubator to turn the eggs and a terrible smell came out.

"PEE U! That stinks!" she cried out as she shut the lid back on the eggs.

Samantha held her nose and took another look inside the incubator. The eggs looked normal. She slowly let her fingers off her nose. She sniffed. GROSS! The terrible smell went up her nose. Samantha shut the lid again just as her mom came in the room to see what the shouting was about.

"Samantha, what's wrong?" her mother asked.

"The incubator stinks!" Samantha replied.

"Oh dear, we have a rotten egg," Mom said, "We have to get it out."
She carefully lifted the lid of the incubator.
Sophie walked in the room and then made a gagging face. "Yuck! What's that smell?" Sophie gasped.

"It's your refrigerator egg," Samantha told her, "It's rotten."

"Ewwwwwww," Sophie said, "So that's what happens when you try to hatch an egg that won't make a chick. At least now we know." Sophie grinned. Samantha hit her forehead with the palm of her hand.

"That's what I told you would happen!" Samantha groaned. She knew that she needed to get the egg out of the incubator. She also didn't want to touch the smelly rotten thing.

"Sophie. It's your refrigerator egg. You get it out," Samantha told her little sister. Sophie looked up at her and made a squelched up face.

"That's gro..." Sophie started to say gross, but Samantha gave her a look and she shut her mouth.

Sophie sighed, "OK." She reached into the incubator and picked up the egg with two fingers. She didn't want to touch it any more than she had too.

As she turned around to take it and put it in the trash can Mom said, "Sophie be very careful not to—'SPLAT'--drop that egg."

The egg had slipped out of Sophie's fingers and had splattered stinky greenish yellow goo all over the kitchen floor. The smell was horrible. It was the most horrible thing Samantha had ever smelled. She felt like she couldn't breathe.

Samantha ran out the back door to try to get away from the smell. It wasn't as strong when she got outside, but it was still super stinky.

Samantha held her nose and ran all the way into the backyard and kept going until she got to the fence surrounding their yard. Surely she was far enough away from the kitchen to be OK now, she thought. She took her fingers off her nose and smelled STINKY ROTTEN EGG! She couldn't get away from it.

That's when Samantha looked down and noticed that some of the rotten egg goo had splattered on her pants. It was on her!

"EWWWWW!" she screamed and started running back towards the house. As soon as she came in the door she held her nose with one hand and started taking off her pants with the other. She had to get away from that smell! She ran past her mom who was in the kitchen cleaning up the rotten egg, dumped her pants in the laundry room and went toward the bathroom to wash off. The door was locked. Samantha banged on the door, but Sophie said, "Go away, I'm washing off rotten egg!"

"You *are* a rotten egg!" Samantha called out as she went to use the bathroom in her parents' room. She jumped in the shower and then put on fresh clothes as fast as she could.

Samantha and Sophie were both tardy for school that morning. Samantha walked into class late and sat down by Gerti. She slipped Gerti a note that said -- Sophie's refrigerator egg was rotten...all others are OK -- Then she started on her morning schoolwork, but every now and again for the rest of the day Samantha kept thinking she got a whiff of rotten egg.

Chapter 6

Growing

Every week Gerti came over after school so they could candle the good eggs together to see how the chicks were growing. They saw them grow from a small dot, no bigger than the eraser on a pencil, to filling up almost the entire egg.

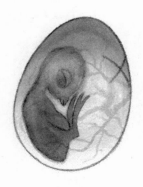

They could even see the babies moving inside the egg. Samantha had read online that the chicks could hear through the shell. The girls also made sure to talk to the eggs whenever they turned them.

One morning, Samantha went to turn the eggs when she noticed Sophie's reddish brown egg had a crack in its shell. At first she was upset because it was still two days before they were due to hatch. She thought something had hit the egg and cracked the shell.

When Sam was looking more closely at the crack, however, she saw movement and heard a little "peep". Samantha carefully laid the egg back down...shut the incubator...and ran as fast as she could calling, "Mom! Moooooooom!"

As she turned the corner to go into the hallway, she almost collided with her mother who was coming to see what she needed.

"Mom. The egg. The chicken. It's hatching!" Samantha could hardly speak, she was so excited.

"What? An egg is hatching? Is it mine?" Sophie asked. She had come to see what the fuss was about when she heard Samantha shouting. Sophie didn't wait for an answer. She ran straight for the incubator. Samantha followed her there, anxious to show off the hatching chick.

Mom came along behind them with Michelle following. As they got to the incubator, Dad came trudging into the room as well.

"Is everyone OK? What's all the ruckus?" he asked sleepily. It was Saturday morning and Dad had proclaimed it a sleep late day for him. He had gotten out of bed when he heard Sam yelling.

"Dad, an egg is hatching, look!" Samantha said, pointing at the incubator. Dad bent down and peeked through the plastic window on the top.

"I don't see it," he said blearily.

"That one there, see that little hole?" Samantha prompted.

Dad squinted and said, "Hmm, looks like I have a few more hours of sleep." Then he kissed the top of Samantha's head and stumbled back down the hall to his bedroom. Mom snickered.

Samantha was not deterred. "We have to call Gerti," she told her mom.

Mom handed Samantha the phone and said, "Gerti is welcome to spend some time over here today. You might as well invite her over. I'll warn you, though, eggs take a long time to hatch. There is no rush."

Sam grabbed the phone and anxiously dialed Gerti's number. "You have to come over right now! The chicks are hatching!" Samantha told her friend. Mom sighed.

Turns out, Mom was right. When Gerti got to Samantha's house the little chick still only had a teeny tiny hole right at the tip of his beak. The girls anxiously peaked in through the window at the top of the incubator every few minutes. The chick didn't seem to be making any progress. It had been a whole ten minutes.

"I think we need to help him," Sophie declared at last.

"We can't Sophie," Samantha replied, "I read about this. The baby chicken needs to struggle to hatch. If we help him, he won't be strong enough to live after he gets out.

"Are you sure?" Gerti asked.

"Yes. We have to wait," Samantha instructed.

"I just wish I could help it. I want to be a good momma chicken," Sophie said sadly.

"The momma chickens chirp to encourage the babies...you could chirp to them," Samantha offered her sister.

"OK. chirp...chirp...chirp," Sophie started making her chirp noise. Then she listened. *chirp* *chirp* They could hear the little chick calling back as it wriggled a little harder. Another piece of shell came off.

"It's working!" Sophie shouted.

"It urkin, it urkin," Michelle mimicked.

While the kids were all crowded around the incubator watching, Mom said, "When this little guy finally does make it out of his shell he's going to need a warm place to live. Who wants to help me make a brooder box?"

"A what?" Sophie said.

"A brooder box. It's a place to keep the chicks warm," Samantha replied. She had been reading all about chickens lately so that she'd know how to take care of the eggs and the baby chicks.

Sam continued, "When the babies are first hatched they can't keep themselves warm. Usually the momma hen uses her feathers to keep them warm under her wings. We are ---"

"We are going to make wings to put the chicks under?" Sophie's face lit up at the thought.

"No."

"We are going to sit in a box and put the chicks under our arms?" Sophie asked hopefully.

"NO."

"We are going get lots of feathers and -"

"NO, NO, NO! Listen to me, will ya? We're going to put a heat lamp over a box to make a warm spot for them," Samantha said quickly before her little sister could interrupt her again.

"Oh," said Sophie mournfully. A box with a light over it did not sound nearly as cool as her ideas.

"That's right, and I know just the box to do the trick," Mom said with a wink. Mom disappeared into the attic and came back holding the same plastic storage tub they used when Gayzer, the box turtle, had visited.

Samantha took newspapers out of the recycling bin and lined the bottom of the brooder box with them. Then she clamped a lamp to the side of the tub and made the light shine down toward the newspapered bottom. With that out of the way, the girls went back to check on the progress of hatching.

Chapter 7

Hatching Out

When they peeked in the incubator again the chick was still struggling and pushing. He almost had a hole large enough to peek through. Samantha, Sophie and Gerti were crowding around to peek in the top.

"Look, another one is hatching," Gerti said as she pointed to the white egg that was marked with an X.

"That one's mine!" Samantha squealed. Relief flooded through her. She had been worried that her eggs would not hatch. She was happy that at least one of them was pipping through. Then Samantha looked over at Gerti. Gerti was looking a little worried herself.

"Don't worry Gert, your eggs will hatch soon I bet," Samantha said, trying to comfort her friend.

"I know. It's just that I would really like to see them come out," Gerti answered.

"Well, Mom says you can stay here all day if you want. You are bound to see your chicks hatch," Samantha assured her.

"Thanks Sam," Gerti said.

Sure enough, the next chick to pip a hole in its shell was one of the teeny little cream eggs of Gerti's. It was followed closely by the other teeny cream egg. Gerti was so excited.

The girls spent the morning checking on the chicks and playing games. Gerti and Samantha agreed that they should play a dancing game. They thought music was a good way to encourage the chicks. Also, it was loads of fun.

Every time a song ended the girls would rush over to the incubator to take a quick peek at the chicks. Ever so slowly, the chicks broke free from their shells.

First they'd start with the teeniest little hole right at the end of their beak. Then they'd keep wiggling and pecking until they had an entire line of shell cracked.

The chicks would wiggle and squirm and push some more until finally they could push the top off of the egg. Then out would tumble a little wet squishy chick.

"Yuck. He looks kinda gross. Why's he so wet?" Sophie asked when the first chick finally made it out of its shell.

Mom laughed when she heard Sophie. "That's how he's supposed to look Sophie. The moisture in the egg keeps the chick healthy when he's inside. Now that he's hatched out we'll leave him in the incubator long enough for him to dry. He'll be fluffy in no time," Mom told her.

Samantha thought he looked beautiful...in a squishy, gross kind of way.

From the eggs she and Gerti had gathered in the farmyard there was a real live baby chick.

It only took a few minutes for the chick to dry off after it got free from its shell. Then it was so cute and fluffy.

After the chick was walking Samantha said, "We'd better get him out of the incubator and put him in the brooder box now. Sophie, this little guy is yours. You want to pick him up?"

Sophie's eyes lit up. "YES!" She exclaimed.

"You have to be very gentle. Cup your hands under him," Samantha guided Sophie through how to hold the chick while she held the incubator open for her little sister.

Sophie was much more careful with the baby chick than she had been with her rotten egg. She slowly and carefully placed the baby chick in the brooder box under the heat lamp.

"I'm going to call her Coconut! Cause she kinda looks like a coconut," Sophie said as she set the chick down.

Mom smiled and said, "I think that's the perfect name Sophie."

When Samantha's chick came out of the shell and was dried off, it was her turn to take it out and put it in the brooder box. "This little guy will be Blaze, because he looks like a blaze of fire," Samantha said.

Next, out of Gerti's two tiny cream eggs came two tiny fluffy chickens. One was solid white, and the other was grey.

"Ooh, you could call the white one Snow," said Sophie.

"Or Snowfoot, because he has white feathers on his feet too," Samantha added.

"What about Abominable?" offered Dad as he walked by. The girls all looked at him quizzically. "Like the abominable snowman," he clarified. Samantha laughed.

"I'm going to call the grey one Shadow and the white one Light," Gerti said.

"I mean, I like your suggestions, but I wanted to name them myself," she added timidly.

"Shadow and Light. Those are great names Gerti," Samantha said. Gerti smiled and then carefully took Shadow and Light and put them under the warm lamp in the brooder box.

Next came Sophie's white egg, which hatched into a little puffy yellow chick that Sophie named Duckiepoo. Duckiepoo was followed by Samantha's reddish brown egg hatching into a reddish brown chick. He was promptly named Squirt.

By the afternoon, only three eggs remained. The girls kept checking on them, but there was no sign of movement. Samantha was starting to realize they probably weren't going to hatch. She looked at them sadly. Then she looked over at the brooder box that was full of life and smiled.

From the hatched eggs there were two tiny, fluffy chicks that were the silkies which had been in Gerti's tiny cream eggs. There were two little puffy yellow chicks from the big white eggs. And two brownish red chicks from the brownish-red eggs. They were all running around in the brooder box cheeping.

Samantha, Sophie, and Gerti all gathered around the brooder box.
Samantha picked up Squirt. Gerti gently scooped up Shadow and Light. Sophie tried to pick up Duckiepoo, but she was going extra slow to be careful. Duckiepoo jumped out of her hands every time she started to

lift him up. Finally Samantha helped Sophie secure the bouncy chick.

"Oh my gosh, they are so cute," Samantha squealed.

"I know, I can't believe how sweet they are," Gerti agreed.

"Ah, she likes it under my shirt," Sophie giggled. Duckipoo had snuggled up under the edge of her shirt and her feathers were tickling Sophie's tummy.

Samantha laughed as she watched Duckipoo stick his head out from under Sophie's shirt.

"Duckipoo loves m-- Hey! Don't bite me! I'm your mama!" said Sophie sternly as her chick pecked at her hand.

"Oh, we need to go get them some food," Samantha said. Samantha had done her research. She knew the chicks still had some nourishment in their bellies from the yolk in the egg. Still, she didn't want them to get hungry before she got food for them.

Just then Sophie squealed again, "Ewww, he pooped on me!"

Samantha looked over and saw Sophie wrinkling her nose in disgust as she held up a hand with a little blob of poop on it. Samantha burst out laughing.

"Oh Sophie, just go wash it off," she said as she picked up Duckipoo and placed him and Squirt back in the brooder box.

Then Samantha went to procure some chick feed.

Chapter 8

New Chick in the Coop

"We need to go to the store and get them some food," Samantha said.

"Come on kid, I'll drop Gerti off at her house and take you to get some chick food. Who else wants to go?" Dad said.

"Me!" Sophie shouted.

"I go, I go too." Michelle chimed in.

"To the car! We should hurry. There is supposed to be a storm blowing in," Dad said as he swooped up Michelle and put her shoes and coat on for her. Samantha grinned and headed out to get in the car.

The weather had turned cold again and Samantha and her sisters were shivering as they piled in the car. "Dad, it's freezing!" Sophie whined.

"Feezing!" Michelle seconded.

"Don't worry we'll get the heat going and be nice and toasty in no time," Dad replied. The car was just getting good and warm when they got to Gerti's house and dropped her off.

"Take good care of the chicks," Gerti said as she got out of the car.

"We will, and you can come see them again soon," Samantha replied.

When they got to the feed store the girls piled out of the car and went walking around looking at saddles and toy tractors and all of the fun stuff that stocked the shelves of a feed and seed store. Dad put a giggling Michelle on his shoulder and dutifully went to find the chick starter feed.

Samantha heard a "peep, peep, peep" sound. She and Sophie followed the sound until she came to a place where there were four huge tubs. They were full of tiny, fluffy, baby chickens.

"Dad!" she called out, "Dad look, it's baby chickens!"

Dad was not impressed.

"We have baby chickens at the house, remember?" he replied.

"There are so many of them. They are so cute!" Sophie practically squealed with delight.

"Alright, you girls can look at the chicks while I buy the food, but be ready to leave when I'm done." Dad said. He put Michelle down so she could look too. "Watch out for Michelle, I'll be right by the counter there," he added.

Sophie and Samantha were trying to decide which one was the cutest when they heard Michelle say sadly, "Chick die. Chick die." Michelle was looking in a different tub than her two sisters.

Samantha went over to where the toddler was pointing and looked. At first she just saw a mass of fluffy chicks running around, but then she saw one little form lying down quietly at the back. A wave of sadness rushed through Samantha at the sight of the chick. She put her arm around Michelle and was going to try to comfort her when Sophie pointed and said, "It moved! It's not dead, it moved!"

Samantha looked again at the little chick, very closely this time. Its eyes fluttered open for just a moment as it tried to raise its head. Then they closed and he lay still again. Samantha didn't even think about it. She reached in and shooed all the other baby chicks away from the hurt one so they wouldn't step on him. Then she very carefully picked him up and held him close to her. "Come on Sophie. Come on

Michelle," Samantha said as she started walking to her Dad.

"Dad we have to buy this one," Samantha told her father as she opened up her hands and showed him the tiny chick lying inside. The little chick feebly lifted his head.

The man behind the counter looked down at the chick Samantha was holding.

"That one doesn't look like it's going to live much longer, Darlin. Why don't you pick out one of the other chicks?" he asked her gently.

Samantha thrust her chin out stubbornly.

"I want this one," she said defiantly, "He'll die without me." In her heart Samantha knew he would probably die with her too, but she also knew she had to try.

Her Dad looked down at her. Then he looked up at the man behind the register and said, "We'll take the chick as well." Dad paid for the injured chick, the chick feed, and a watering jar. Samantha thought she heard him grumbling something about no more animals ever in his house. He grumbled that a lot.

They all marched out of the store with Samantha cradling the chick as carefully as she could in her hands. When they arrived home and walked in the door, Dad announced, "We have one more for the brood." Mom looked up at him, then down at Samantha's hands. She smiled.

"Let me see here," Mom said as she gently took the chick from Samantha. Mom was as big a sucker for animals as Samantha was. The chick lifted her head and made a tiny peep sound. Mom set her down gently on the floor and though the chick tried to stand up, she immediately fell on her side again.

"Samantha," Mom said solemnly, "We'll do what we can for it, but you need to know it's probably going to die." A tear rolled down Samantha's cheek. Sophie and Michelle crowded in, listening as well.

Mom got a little wire cage and set it inside the bigger brooder box that had the other chicks in it. She lay newspaper on the bottom and put a little dish of water and a little dish of food as well. "Put the chick in here and she can see the other chickens. She'll also be safe from being stepped on by them," Mom said.

Mom adjusted the heat lamp so that all the chicks could get enough heat and added food and water for the rest of the chicks as well.

"Alright, Samantha. He doesn't look like he'll make it, but we are giving him a fighting chance," Mom said.

"Thanks Mom. Thanks Dad," Samantha said as she gave her mom and dad a hug. Sophie did the same thing. Outside the wind was howling. Samantha shivered. She was glad her chicks were safe and warm inside. The rest of the evening Samantha checked on the chicks every few minutes.

After dinner that night, the little hurt chick was still alive.

"I think I'll name her Slingshot, because her neck is a little crooked," Samantha said.

"I think that's a great name. If Slingshot makes it through the night it will be a good sign. The most important thing we can do is just to keep her warm," Mom told Samantha. Samantha double-checked the heat lamp and made sure Slingshot and the other chicks were warm enough.

"Hang in there, Slingshot," Samantha whispered as she headed to bed.

Chapter 9

Power Outage

That night, Samantha was awakened by the sound of a siren going off. Her parents came in and told her to get out of bed. Dad was scooping up Sophie. Mom had Michelle in her arms as she told Samantha, "You need to come into the hallway for a little while. There are tornadoes coming."

Samantha sleepily crawled out of bed and into the hallway. Mom had made a pallet out of some blankets and they laid down the still sleeping Sophie and Michelle.

"Here you go honey, go back to sleep. There are bad storms around. We just wanted to be in the hallway because it's a little bit safer," Mom assured her.

Samantha tried to lie back down, but she could hear the rain pounding and the thunder booming outside.

"Dad, can the chicks come into the hallway too?" she asked.

"Sure, I'll go grab them," Dad replied and headed off to the living room to collect the chicks. Samantha wanted to check on Slingshot and make sure she was still OK. When Dad got back, Sam went over to the brooder box and was relieved to see that

Slingshot was still breathing. She even looked a little stronger when she tried to raise her head up. Samantha was starting to feel better when she heard a loud POP. The lights went out.

"Eek!" Samantha screamed. Sophie and Michelle were still snoring obliviously. Mom always said they could sleep through anything. Guess it was true. The hallway had gone completely dark.

"Don't worry. The power is out, but I've got a lantern right here," Mom said as she pulled out their camping lantern and turned it on. Having light made Sam feel better. Until she realized it wasn't just the hallway lights that had gone out. The heat light was dark as well.

"Mom, the chicks don't have heat. They need heat or they'll die!" Samantha said. That's when Sophie woke up.

"Die? They have heat, don't they? What's going on?" she yawned.

"The power is out, and the heat lamp is off, and the baby chicks are only a day old and if they get cold they'll die," Samantha was getting herself upset.

"Calm down, honey," Mom said gently, "The power doesn't usually stay off for long. Why don't we all make a tent with some blankets around us and the chicks? It'll trap our body heat and help keep everyone warm until the power comes back on."

Dad and Samantha went to grab extra blankets off of all the beds.

Samantha grabbed every blanket in the house. She came back down the hall carrying a pile of blankets as tall as she was. Everyone snuggled close beside the brooder box as Dad draped the blankets over their heads.

All the healthy chicks in the box had started huddling together to stay warm. Slingshot was all alone in her spot. Samantha reached in and gently picked her up. She held her close to her to try to share her warmth.

They sat there a long time that way. The storm passed, but the power did not come back on. The blankets kept them warm for a little while. The longer the power was out, the colder it seemed to get inside the house. Samantha pulled her arms inside her shirt and cupped Slingshot in her hands next to her stomach to try to keep her warm with body heat. Mom, Dad, and Sophie each took two chicks and held them close as well. Samantha kept thinking about Mom's warning that the most important thing to help Slingshot stay alive was to keep her warm. She wondered what else she could do. If she didn't find a way to get warmer, Slingshot would die.

If only she could just have Dad turn the heat up like he did in the car earlier that day.   That's it, Samantha thought...the car! "Mom, Dad! There is heat in the car. We can keep the chicks warm that way!" Samantha told them.

Samantha's Mom and Dad looked at each other. Dad shrugged and said, "The danger has passed. It's a good idea until we get the power back on. I'll go start the car." Dad gently set the chicks he had been holding back in the brooder box.

Samantha grinned. "Hold on little guys, we are going to get you warmed up," she whispered.

While Dad was out getting the car warmed up, Mom had found a box big enough to put the chicks in and set a towel inside. Then they carefully settled all of the healthy chicks in the box to cuddle together. The chicks peeped and snuggled close to each other. Samantha kept Slingshot.

When Dad returned he picked up Michelle first, wrapped her in a blanket and carried her out to the car. Sophie was right behind him. Samantha carried Slingshot and her Mom carried the box with the other baby chicks in it. They all got settled in the car, and Dad pulled out of the driveway.

"We might as well drive around a bit and see what kind of damage this storm dealt," he said. The car was cool at first, but as they drove around the block the heat started to kick in. Samantha felt herself relax a bit. She knew the chicks would survive the night. They drove around in the warm car until the power came back on. By morning the danger had passed. All

seven chicks were alive and Slingshot was
even sitting up on her own.

Chapter 10

Backyard Chickens

Three weeks later the chicks were quickly outgrowing the brooder box in the dining room. Samantha leaned over to pick up Squirt. He hopped up on her happily. She knew it would be time to find homes for them soon. Her mom had told her from the beginning that they had to go to the farm. As Samantha looked down at the little chick perched on her arm, she wanted to keep him so badly.

While Samantha sat mulling over the problem, Sophie walked in.

"I don't want to give them away," Sophie said exactly what Samantha had been thinking. Sophie continued, "I think we should keep them in our clubhouse in the back yard and hide them in there. If no one knows we have them then they can't take them away right?"

"Mom and Dad would know," Samantha said sadly.

"What if we just saved Duckipoo. We could definitely hide at least one!" Sophie decided.

"Sophie, you don't think Mom would notice that one of the chicks went missing and our clubhouse started chirping?" Samantha said sourly.

"Well, what's your great idea then?" Sophie retorted.

Samantha thought about it for a moment. Sophie was right, they had to try something. When Samantha had been researching how to care for the eggs and chicks she found lots of stories about people who kept chickens in their backyards. The trick was going to be to convince her Mom and Dad that it would work for them.

"OK. We are going to try Operation Save The Chickens," Samantha declared.

"Yes!" Sophie whooped as she jumped up in the air.

"First, we need to show Mom and Dad why it would be good to keep them," Samantha instructed.

"That's easy, because they are sooooooo cute!" Sophie said.

"Yeah, but cute doesn't work on Mom. She *would* like the fresh eggs they will lay when they are older, though," Samantha replied.

"OK, but also they are soooooo cute," said Sophie. Samantha rolled her eyes at her little sister, but she had to agree. Her chickens were terribly cute.

"Next step is to be ready for Mom and Dad's arguments. They will say things like we don't have a cage for them. Or they might say they are a lot of work to take care of," Samantha instructed her sister.

"I've already worked the cage out...we can use the clubhouse," Sophie grinned.

"They would poop on it," Samantha pointed out.

"Oh yeah," Sophie grimaced.

"But I think I have another plan....Grampi," Samantha said triumphantly. Grampi lived next door and had a workshop behind his house. He was always looking for things to build and had lots of scrap lumber to make a chicken coop with.

The girls spent the rest of the afternoon drawing up coop plans, making lists, and getting ready to discuss the prospect of keeping the chickens with their parents. At dinner time Samantha and Sophie gave their presentation to Mom and Dad.

Everything was going well until Mom pointed out that roosters weren't allowed in the city. Apparently, not everyone appreciates being awakened by a rooster crowing loudly.

"It figures it's the boys that are trouble," Samantha said sourly.

"Tell you what, Samantha. *If* your Grampi is willing to help you build a coop, and *if* you girls are willing to feed and water the chickens *every* day, then we could let the hens stay," Mom conceded.

"How do we know which ones are girls and which are the boy chickens, though?" Samantha asked. She wanted to keep as many as she could.

"That's easy," Dad chimed in, "When they get older, the ones that lay eggs are hens and the ones that crow are roosters." Samantha grinned. She hoped they would never crow.

As soon as dinner was over the girls bolted over to Grampi's house to get him in on the plan. "Grampi, we need your help building something," Samantha told him when they walked in the door.

"Oh really? What kind of something?" Grampi asked.

"A chicken coop," the girls replied.

"Mom says we can keep the chickens, but you've got to build us a coop," Samantha added.

Grampi grinned, "Got to, eh?"

"Well, 1 hope you will. Please?" Samantha said.

"Yeah. Pleeeeeeeeeese. With cherries on top," Sophie added.

"Well, what kind of coop did you ladies have in mind?" Grampi asked.

Samantha and Sophie showed Grampi the plans they had drawn. They had looked at lots of pictures of backyard chicken coops to get their ideas.

"The important things for a coop," Samantha explained to Grampi, "are a safe place for the hens to sleep at night, a place for them to be on the ground in the daytime and a place for them to lay eggs."

"And it has to be strong enough to keep predators out. Rowrrl," Sophie said with a growl for emphasis.

"Predators?" Grampi asked.

"Yeah, things that would try to eat the chickens. Like a bear!" Sophie told Grampi happily.

"Well, more like a raccoon or a possum," Samantha said.

"A bear could eat a chicken," Sophie defended.

"But we don't have any bears in town!" Samantha countered.

"Oh yeah," said Sophie.

"OK. We need to keep out predators. Raccoons, opposums, and bears," Grampi said with a wink. Sophie grinned triumphantly. Samantha giggled.

They spent a few more minutes going over their plans with Grampi. Then they went out to the shed to look for materials they could use. Grampi kept a pile of scrap wood that was left-over from his other projects. They were able to find almost everything they needed to make the coop.

Samantha and Sophie were still scrounging

around the shop looking for some wheels to make the coop moveable when Mom called them home to get ready for bed.

"Don't worry girls. I'll get started and you can help me work on the chicken coop after school tomorrow," Grampi told them. Samantha went to bed smiling.

The next day after they got home from school the girls finished their homework as fast as they could so they could go help Grampi. They went to work straight away on building the coop. It was lots of fun working with Grampi. He let the girls use the power screwdriver and hammer the nails. After they had been working for a while Gran came out to check on their progress. She brought snacks and ice water.

"Thanks Gran," the girls said as they each took an apple slice spread with peanut butter. Grampi went for the ice water first.

"Your Gran is the best," Grampi told the girls as he drank the entire glass of ice water. After their snack break, everyone went back to work. Gran even stayed and helped awhile until Mom called for the girls to come home.

The next afternoon when the girls got to Grampi's house he had the coop all put together. It was sitting on the ground with newspaper under the entire thing.

"You know what this coop needs?" he asked the girls. "Paint!" he said, answering his own question as he held up two paintbrushes. Samantha and Sophi grinned. They loved to paint.

Grampi had set out three different paint cans on the table. "These are some leftover paints I had that will keep the rain off the wood," Grampi told them. The girls started painting the coop while Grampi searched one more time for those wheels.

"I know I have them around here someplace. I saved them off of an old wagon," he said.

"Ah Ha! Got em," Grampi said triumphantly and brought the wheels over. The girls had just about finished painting.

"You girls go home and let this paint dry and we'll have this coop ready for chickens tomorrow," Grampi assured them.

Chapter 11

No Crowing Allowed

It was a good thing the coop was almost ready. The chickens were growing bigger each day and were getting crowded in their brooder box. Samantha was especially proud of how well Slingshot was doing. Other than a crook in her neck, she was as healthy as all the other chicks. The problem was, the chicks were also getting noisy. Samantha's Dad had started threatening to have chicken for dinner one night if they stayed any longer. So

Samantha was glad when the next afternoon Gerti came home from school with them and they moved the chickens out to the backyard.

Every morning after that Samantha let the chickens out of the shed portion and into the yard of the coop. In the afternoons the girls would go outside and let the chickens out of the coop and into the backyard to play. One such afternoon while they were out playing, Samantha saw Squirt find a bug. He grabbed it in his beak and took off running across the yard. All the other chickens took up the chase and ran after him to take his prize. He thought he had gotten away when Duckipoo came up from behind and took the bug away from

him. Squirt was upset. As he watched
Duckipoo gulp down his prey he stretched
out and gave an angry "Er er er errrr" crow.

Samantha froze. She had known that
some of her chickens were probably
roosters. She had known it was coming,
but she didn't want it to be Squirt. He was
the goofiest, funniest of them all. He was
her favorite. Maybe she was wrong and
that wasn't really a crow, she told herself.
But the next day, it happened again.

In fact, it seemed like once Squirt
started crowing, he wanted to crow all the
time. Not only that, but Duckipoo started
crowing too. It didn't take long before
Mom heard them as well.

"You know they have to go to the farm, Samantha," Mom said.

"I know," Sam said sadly.

"Grandpa said he'll come get them and the roosters can live at their farm. At least you'll be able to visit them," Mom said.

Grandpa came up that weekend to pick up Squirt and Duckipoo. "Girls these are some 'egg'ceptional chickens," Grandpa said trying to lighten the mood. The girls didn't even grin. Grandpa picked up Squirt, and stuck the chicken's legs out in front of him saying, "It was quite a "feet" to raise them. HA!"

Samantha grinned at that one. Mostly because Grandpa looked funny holding Squirt that way.

Sophie said, "I don't get it."

"A feat is doing something impressive. Grandpa was switching the words around with chicken feet," Samantha started explaining to her. Squirt chose that moment to go to the bathroom and it landed on Grandpa's arm.

"Oh, POOP!" Grandpa said with mock horror on his face. Both girls laughed this time.

Samantha was sad to see her chicken go, but she felt better about Squirt going with Grandpa. When it came time for him to go, Samantha put Squirt in the carrier.

"Goodbye buddy. I know you are going to like it on the farm, but I'll miss you," she told him.

Sophie put Duckipoo in as well and told him, "I'll come visit soon."

A week later Samantha and Sophie were out playing in the yard with the chickens that were left. Sam had been listening carefully to see if Blaze, Coconut, Slingshot or Shadow and Light would start crowing, but so far none had.

Samantha grabbed Shadow and put her on Sophie's head. She balanced there precariously as Sophie laughed, "Samantha, get her off before she poops on my head!"

"Just shake your head silly," Samantha said. Sophie shook her head gently and Shadow flapped her wings wildly as she jumped to the ground squawking in protest. The girls giggled.

"How do you think Squirt and Duckipoo are doing?" Sophie asked Samantha.

"I bet they are kings of the farm," Samantha replied. She knew Sophie missed Duckipoo as much as she missed Squirt.

"This might help," Mom said. She had just walked out the back door of the house and was holding up an envelope. It was from Grandma and Grandpa and was addressed to Samantha and Sophie. Samantha opened it up and inside there was a picture and a note. The picture showed Duckipoo happily perched on a fence. In front of the fence stood a goat and standing on the goat's back was a rather proud looking Squirt.

The note said, "The roosters are ruling the farmyard around here. We can't wait to see what animal you'll find next. --Love Grandma and Grandpa."

The End

This story was inspired by many different encounters with chickens. They are one of those fun creatures that are very commonplace and yet often overlooked. When little girls don't collect the eggs, several hens will often contribute eggs to one nest. When they have about 12 eggs laid, one of the hens will "go broody".

This hen is responsible for incubating and caring for the eggs. She will use her body heat to keep the eggs warm. She also turns the eggs regularly. If anyone tries to disturb her she will get angry and protest loudly. This hen rarely gets up even to eat and drink for the 21 days it takes to incubate the eggs.

Once the eggs hatch she leads the chicks to food and water. The chicks follow her around and stay under the mother hen's protection until they are large enough to fend for themselves. In our story Samantha, Sophie and Gerti took the place of the "mother hen".

To read some true stories of chickens that inspired this book go to www.SamsAnimals.info.

Quiz Time

Were you paying attention? All the answers to these questions are in the story...

Why was Sally carrying a camera around her neck at the 4-H meeting?

What did Sally want to show Samantha and Gerti?

How many eggs did Samantha and Gerti find on the farm?

Why did Samantha want to put the eggs on the windowsill?

At what temperature did the chicken eggs need to incubate in order to hatch?

Why did the girls keep water in the incubator?

What did Sophie put in the incubator?

Why did the girls need to roll the eggs each day?

How did the girls check to see if the chicks were growing inside the eggs?

Why couldn't Samantha get away from the rotten egg smell?

Why did Samantha pick up Slingshot at the feedstore?

What did Sophie want to make instead of a brooder box to keep the chicks warm?

Why did Squirt and Duckipoo get sent to the farm?

Chicken Fun Facts

- There are dozens of different breeds of chickens. White Leghorns, Silkies, Rhode Island Reds and Dominickers were used as inspiration in this story.

- Different breeds of chickens lay different color eggs. Egg colors can be shades of white, brown, green or blue. Some even have speckles.

- Chickens are omnivores and will eat almost anything small enough to get in their mouths. They might eat such things as seeds, leaves, insects, and even small lizards.

- Chickens are good at searching for their food and will scratch at the ground to uncover insects, worms, and other yummy morsels.

- Female (girl) chickens are called hens when they are old enough to lay eggs. They are called pullets when they are younger.

- Male (boy) chickens are called roosters or cockerels.

- Baby chickens are called chicks.

- Hens will lay eggs even without a rooster around. The eggs will not hatch, however, unless there has been a rooster with the hen to fertilize the eggs.

- Chicken eggs usually take around 21 days to hatch after they start incubating. A few days more or less is also normal.

- Chickens like to keep themselves clean and will preen their feathers with their beak every day.

- Chickens live in flocks and will help each other to set on eggs and raise young.

atch for the next book in the Samantha Series!

SAMANTHA
Plays Possum

About the Author
Daisy Griffin

When she is not rescuing animals from the many things they can get into on their own, she and her husban are raising children, who are as much or more interested creatures as she is. While all the Samantha Stories are works of fiction they all start with an animal found in real life.

www.SamsAnimals.info

About the Illustrator
Matthew Gauvin

Matthew was born in St. Johnsbury Vermont and ent five years in Boston studying at Massachussetts llege of Art and Design. In his short career he's strated twelve books and won a number of art awards. now lives in East Burke Vermont with his wife Barb. ey have a Beagle named Biscuit alternately known as og Dog", for his uncanny ability to look like a frog with back legs sprawled out behind him, a cross eyed cat ned Snowball, a klutzy cat named Tigger, and a cat ned Whicket, affectionately nicknamed "Sticky Whicky" all the times he got stuck up a sappy pine tree.

www.MatthewGauvin.com

Made in the USA
Lexington, KY
10 March 2013